A Teddy Bear's Picnic

Original stories about teddy bears

Illustrated by Terry Denton

Melbourne
Oxford University Press
Oxford Auckland New York

OXFORD UNIVERSITY PRESS

Oxford New York Toronto
Delhi Bombay Calcutta Madras Karachi
Petaling Jaya Singapore Hong Kong Tokyo
Nairobi Dar es Salaam Cape Town
Melbourne Auckland
and associated companies in
Berlin Ibadan

© This collection Oxford University Press 1986
© Illustrations Terry Denton 1986
First published 1986
Reprinted in this edition 1989

National Library of Australia
Cataloguing-in-Publication data:

A Teddy bear's picnic.
ISBN 0 19 554979 1

1. Children's stories, Australian. 2. Teddy bears –
Juvenile fiction. I. Denton Terry.

A823'.30809282

Designed by Terry Denton
Typeset in 16 point Cheltenham Book by Bookset, Melbourne
Printed in Hong Kong
Published by Oxford University Press,
253 Normanby Road, South Melbourne
OXFORD is a trademark of Oxford University Press

Contents

The Little Brown Bear

Robin Klein

The toy shop in Dorset Street was so busy that often the window display didn't get changed for weeks on end. That's how the little brown bear became faded by the sun. He was put in a corner of the window and the shop people forgot all about him.

When they finally changed the display, the assistant said, 'Oh, look what's happened to this little bear!'

'Mark him "half price" and put him on the damaged goods shelf,' said the manager. 'Though it isn't likely that anyone will buy him. He's not what you'd call a very pretty bear.'

The little brown bear was put on the damaged goods shelf with a scratched train set and a Jack-in-the-box whose spring had snapped. During shop hours, many hands picked him up, but dropped him again, because he wasn't a very pretty bear. The seam of an ear came loose and the faded tartan ribbon around his neck lost its bow. Because of all those careless hands picking him up and dropping him again, he also lost his growl. People bought the train set and the Jack-in-the-box, thinking they were getting a wonderful bargain, but nobody was interested in the shabby little bear.

Gradually he was pushed further and further along the shelf, into a dark corner. He ended up on his head, as silent as a broken bell. Dust settled on his fur and his lopsided eyes looked rather sadly out upon the world upside down.

The shop grew busier and busier, for it was school holidays. One day three children came in with their aunt, who spoiled them all dreadfully and talked a lot. 'You can choose any toy you like,' she said grandly. 'I don't care how much it costs.'

The eldest child (who was called Tracey and who wasn't very nice) ran all around the shop trying on roller skates and bouncing beach balls, even though

6

there was a sign saying not to. Finally she came back with the biggest and zappiest electronic game she could find, and didn't even say thank you nicely to her aunt for buying it.

The middle child (whose name was Roger and who wasn't very nice, either) ran about the shop rattling boxes of jigsaw-puzzle pieces, snatching cars out of displays and not putting them back properly, and complaining that there weren't enough animals in the farm sets. He finally came back with a noisy armoured tank that could be worked by remote control. He didn't say thank you, either, but demanded to go straight home because he wanted to show it off to all his friends.

'Amelia hasn't chosen anything yet,' said the aunt. (Amelia was the youngest child, and she wasn't a bit like the others.)

'Oh, *her!*' said Tracey and Roger. 'Just get her anything. She's too little and silly to choose a toy by herself. Don't you know she can't even talk properly yet!'

But Amelia (who could talk very well when she wanted to, but hardly ever got the chance with a brother and sister like that) walked carefully around the shop looking at things.

'How about this big red and silver drum?' said the aunt. 'How about a big set of skittles?'

'You got her one of those last time you took us out,' said Tracey crossly. 'She never even plays with it. Make her hurry up!'

The aunt took expensive and glamorous toys down from the shelves and showed them all to Amelia, but Amelia politely shook her head. There were lots of similar toys in her house, and most of them had been  broken by Roger and Tracey, fighting over whose turn it was.

'Don't let her buy anything if she's going to be so slow,' said Roger. 'I want to go home and play with my tank!'

'It's no use getting her

that telephone set, because she can't talk properly,' Tracey said nastily.

But Amelia didn't really want the telephone set, any-how. She looked along the shelves at all the sparkling toys, and right at the end of the last shelf was the little brown bear, gazing at the world upside down. Gazing right into her eyes.

Amelia slowly reached out and picked him up and inspected him.

'Fancy choosing anything as ugly as that!' Roger jeered. 'Aunty, we told you she was too silly to choose a toy all by herself. She's so silly she never even talks!'

Amelia opened her mouth to say something, but Tracey burst in. 'Dumb bear!' she scoffed. 'Look at its ear with all the stuffing trickling out! And the ribbon's not even tied properly. Aunty, tell her to hurry up, be-cause I want to get home and play with my electronic game!'

Amelia gently tied the frayed tartan ribbon around the little bear's neck back into a bow.

'Amelia, you can have that odd little bear if you like, but wouldn't you rather have a nice scooter with a horn?' asked the aunt.

'It's no use asking *her* anything,' said Tracey. 'She never talks. She's just as dumb as that bear. Ugly old thing it is, and look, it hasn't even got a growl! What's the use of a teddy bear without a growl?'

Amelia opened her mouth. 'That's ...' she whispered, but Roger and Tracey and the aunt didn't listen. The aunt was paying for the three toys, and Tracey and Roger were pushing and shoving and fighting and squabbling in the shop doorway, each trying to get out first.

'Come along, Amelia,' said the aunt over her shoulder, not waiting for an answer.

'... that's why I like him,' Amelia whispered to the empty air. 'Because he doesn't make any noise! He just ... listens.'

And the little brown bear looked at her with his bright eyes, willing to listen forever.

Tom Teddy

June Epstein

Tom Teddy was a present when Jonathan was a baby. He was nearly as big as Jonathan, but Jonathan grew and grew while Tom Teddy stayed the same size.

There was a key in his back, and when it was wound up music played inside him. After a time the key jammed and the music didn't play any more. A seam came loose on his tummy so that the stuffing showed. But Jonathan didn't care because Tom Teddy was his friend. He took him to bed every night.

One day Jonathan's cousin Ben came to play. They took Tom Teddy into the sandpit for a picnic, and they climbed up the slide and slid down. They took turns on Jonathan's tricycle until it started to rain.

That night at bedtime Tom Teddy was nowhere to be found.

Dad went out to the sandpit with an umbrella and a torch but he couldn't find Tom Teddy.

'We'll have to wait until morning,' he told Jonathan.

Jonathan had to go to bed without Tom Teddy.

Next morning, as soon as he woke up, he ran outside and looked in the sandpit. He looked under the slide and everywhere in the garden. He looked in the house.

No one could find Tom Teddy that day, or the next, or the next.

Some days later Jonathan was playing in the sandpit when he heard a squawking, fluttering sound. A big bird flew down past his head, into a thick bush. Soon it came out with something white in its beak, and flew up into a tree.

Down it came again, and then back to the tree with something in its beak. Then another bird flew down.

'I wonder what they're doing,' said Jonathan to himself. He looked into the bush and saw something white and brown.

It was Tom Teddy!

The birds had found the holes in his tummy and were pecking out the stuffing.

'Go away!' shouted Jonathan.

He tried to reach into the bush but his arm was too short and the bush was prickly.

The birds fluttered around his head.

'Shoo! Shoo!' shouted Jonathan.

Dad heard him and came out to see what was happening.

'I've found Tom Teddy,' said Jonathan, 'but I can't reach him, and the birds are taking his stuffing away.'

'They're using it to line their nests,' said Dad.

Dad's arm was longer than Jonathan's so he reached into the bush and pulled out Tom Teddy. Tom Teddy was wet and his fur stuck up in little points, but Jonathan hugged him tightly.

'How ever did he get into that bush?' asked Dad. 'You must have dropped him when you were on the slide.'

'I *didn't*!' said Jonathan.

'Maybe Ben did,' said Dad.

'Can you mend him?' asked Jonathan.

'Of course. Now there's a big hole I can see the little box that makes the music, and I think we'll be able to fix it. Let's give this old stuffing to the birds and get some new clean stuff for Tom Teddy.'

Jonathan pulled out the old stuffing and threw it in the bush for the birds, while Dad fetched a screwdriver.

They fixed the music box, then they dried Tom Teddy, filled him with clean new stuffing, and mended the hole. Jonathan brushed Tom Teddy's fur until it was smooth again.

'When the birds have finished their nests they'll lay eggs and baby birds will hatch,' said Dad.

That night Jonathan pretended his bed was a warm nest. He cuddled up to Tom Teddy, turned the key and went to sleep listening to the music.

Elephant's Lunch

Kate Walker

Clara Bear stared into her school bag and frowned.

'Are you sure you've given me enough lunch?' she asked her mother.

'Enough?' her mother cried. 'You've got four peanut-butter sandwiches, six bananas, a big piece of cherry cake and a whole apple pie.'

'But I'll be at school *all* day,' said Clara, 'and I get *awfully* hungry, especially in the afternoons.'

'Then don't eat all your food in the morning,' said her mother. 'Save some for the afternoon.'

'But I get *awfully* hungry in the mornings, too,' said Clara.

'You won't get hungry,' said her mother. 'You

couldn't possibly get hungry. You've got enough lunch in there to fill an elephant. Now off you go.'

'All right,' said Clara Bear, 'if you say so.'

She kissed her mother goodbye and set off for school.

As she was walking by the railway line Clara saw an elephant. He was standing on the other side of the tracks. Clara stopped and looked at him. The elephant stared back.

'Hello,' she said.

The elephant blinked its small, wrinkled eyes and looked away along the railway tracks.

'Are you waiting for a train?' she asked. The elephant didn't answer. There were no trains in sight.

'I waited for a train once,' said Clara, 'and it was late and I got *awfully* hungry. So hungry my tummy got angry and growled and made a pain. I hope your train isn't late because your tummy is much much bigger than mine and you'll get a terrible pain.'

Clara knew that elephants liked peanuts so she opened her bag, unwrapped her peanut-butter sandwiches and held one out to him.

'You can have it all, if you like,' she said but the elephant just stared. 'It's peanut-butter — yummy yummy!' Clara rubbed her tummy to show the elephant what she meant, but he didn't understand.

'It's yummy to eat,' she said, and bit into the sandwich making loud, enjoyable munching sounds until it

was all gone. Then she held out the second sandwich to him. But the elephant just stared as before.

Clara Bear munched her way through the second sandwich, saying, 'Yummy yummy.' She ate the third one, saying, 'Mmmm! Mmmm!' and licking her lips. But still the elephant didn't understand.

She held out the fourth sandwich. 'If you don't eat this last yummy, peanut-butter sandwich, I will,' she warned. The elephant didn't blink, he didn't even wiggle his ears.

'This is your last chance then.' Clara raised the sandwich to her mouth. 'And this is your second last chance.' She opened her mouth wide. She even gave him a third-last chance, but the elephant looked away.

'Gone!' said Clara, taking an enormous bite. The sandwich disappeared.

Licking the peanut-butter off her paws Clara said,

'You may not know this, elephant, but trains can be late, so late in fact that sometimes they don't come at all. Imagine how hungry you're going to be then. If you don't eat something you'll be sorry.'

Clara opened her bag again and took out the six bananas. Elephants liked bananas, she knew that, so she peeled them one by one and laid them out for the elephant to take. But he looked away again, not interested.

Maybe it wasn't elephants that liked bananas. Now that they were peeled they couldn't go back into the bag. They would have to be eaten. And Clara was the only one there to eat them so she sat down and munched away at all six of them.

'You'll be sorry when your train doesn't come and you get a big pain,' Clara told the elephant. She peered into her bag again. 'I suppose you like cherry cake?'

Silly question. Everybody in the whole world liked cherry cake. Especially cherry cake with chocolate icing and rainbow sprinkles.

Clara Bear looked along the railway track. There was still no train in sight. She looked at the elephant with his awfully big tummy.

'All right,' she said at last, 'I'll share my cake with you.'

She broke the cherry cake in half, and placed one piece on the railway track for the elephant to take. She went to put the other piece back in her bag, but

couldn't resist taking just one small bite. Then another. And because it was so yummy, just one more, until there was only one bite left. And there didn't seem much point in putting just one bite of cake away, so she ate that too.

Then in the distance she heard a train coming. It had to be the elephant's train, of course. He wouldn't go hungry after all! Clara Bear quickly picked up the other piece of cherry cake and backed well away to watch the train go through.

Sure enough it pulled up, stood still for a minute, then blew its whistle and moved off again, clicking and swaying down the line.

The elephant was gone. And when Clara looked down, so was the other piece of cherry cake. Only a smear of chocolate icing and a few sprinkles remained on her paw. She'd eaten it without thinking while watching the train go through. Now all she had left for an entire day's lunch was one, not very big, apple pie with short-crust pastry and cinnamon on top.

'Oh dear, I'm going to get *awfully* hungry at school,' she thought. 'Just like the time I waited for the train and it was late. My tummy will get angry and growl and give me a pain.'

Clara made a quick decision. To make her bag as light as possible she gobbled down the apple pie with the short-crust pastry and cinnamon on top and ran all the way home.

'Mummy,' she ran into the kitchen out of breath, 'I need some more lunch, quickly.' She opened her empty school bag.

Her mother stared into it with wide eyes. 'Clara, what happened to the lunch I gave you?'

'I ate it,' said Clara. 'I had to. There was this elephant waiting for his train and he was very worried about getting hungry . . .'

'I see,' said her mother, nodding her head. 'So it was an elephant today?'

'That's right,' said Clara.

'Not a rhinoceros?' said her mother.

'No,' said Clara, 'the rhinoceros was yesterday.'

'And not a giraffe?'

'No. I met the giraffe the day before,' Clara Bear smiled.

Mother Bear shook her head and started to pack another lunch: another four peanut-butter sandwiches, six bananas, a big piece of cherry cake and another apple pie with cinnamon.

'Do you think I could have an apple as well,' said Clara, 'just in case?'

'Clara, where do you put all this food?' said her mother.

'In my tummy, of course,' said Clara, 'so it won't growl at me and make a pain. I wouldn't put it anywhere else.'

'Well, I'm sorry to have to say this,' said her mother a little annoyed, 'but you eat like an elephant.'

'That's not true!' said Clara. 'I eat much more than elephants. They're just like rhinoceroses, they don't eat anything at all.'

Next day on her way to school Clara met a camel and found that camels don't eat very much either.

Teddy Bears' Picnic

Dorothy Rickards

'Picnic! Picnic!' is the shout,
So Mumma gets the basket out.
Dadda must have been out fishing —
It smells too bad to put a dish in.

Rodney Bear takes out the bread,
He finds a knife and starts to spread;
In the fridge — he finds too late —
The soap was on the butter plate.

Belinda Bear then makes a cake;
As well, she makes a sad mistake.
It comes out flat in half-an-hour —
She put in salt instead of flour.

23

Grandpa Bear just sits and knits
Until young cousin Archie trips;
Grandpa's quite upset, of course,
To have his whiskers splashed with sauce.

Baby Bear starts packing up.
Crash! Well, that's a broken cup.
Whose pawmark is it in the jam?
The jelly's squashed, and so's the ham.

Ralph reaches for the honey pot
To pack as well, but quite a lot
Of honey trickles on his head,
So he sits and licks it up instead.

Dadda Bear gets out the car;
Alas! He doesn't get too far.
Whatever is that horrid row?
(The garage door is open, now!)

Says Dadda Bear, 'I've had enough!
I'm done with all this picnic stuff!'
He sits down on a kitchen chair
And says they'll all have dinner there.

One Teddy Too Many

Michael Janover

The night was hot. It was raining and Boswell the teddy bear felt left out. There was nothing unusual for Boswell in feeling left out. He was a small, brown, ragged teddy in a world full of big, pink teddies with bright noses, wide grins and knitted suits.

Boswell waited and waited to be played with and dressed up by his owner, a pink-faced little girl named Carlotta Pamplemousse. But somehow when it came to being played with, dressed up, taught cooking or talking, Boswell was always left in the green corner where the toys were kept while all the other bears basked in the rosy light of chubby Carlotta's fun and games. Boswell looked out the window at the drizzly sky and a little tear drizzled slowly down his cheek.

Hardly anybody was left in the green corner tonight. The pink teddies had all gone to the circus in Carlotta's basket. Carlotta loved the circus and she always took

her favourite toys with her like a queen taking her ladies-in-waiting with her to court. Rebecca her red-eyed doll and Aladdin her Arabian Nights doll, and Twisty the snake, and Polly, Parsley and Pip, her chirpy pink teddies all went to the circus in Carlotta's basket. Polly, Parsley and Pip fell asleep every time. Boswell thought they slept all the time because they were so lazy and stupid. Rebecca the red-eyed doll eyed the camels with suspicion. And Aladdin spent the evening wrapped in Carlotta's white cardigan, bored by the circus.

Boswell would have given his jacket to go to the circus. And he did love his jacket — it was red and white checks and made him feel like playing the trumpet whenever he looked at himself in the mirror. But he was always left out.

'You are just one teddy too many!' Carlotta had said sternly as she tossed Boswell into the green corner where he now lay. Nobody was left except a few old building blocks he hardly knew: Tor and Slab and Brick were their names and they didn't say much.

Rebecca's doll-house stood empty in the middle of the room. Boswell looked out sadly on this lonely

scene. Then he caught sight of his friend. At first Boswell only heard his friend who lay on his side behind Rebecca's doll-house. But Boswell knew who it was by the sound of the snoring.

'Chester! Chester!' Boswell called.

And slowly, softly a reply came from the apple-green and banana-yellow giraffe who lay on the blue carpet.

'Hullo, Boz, old chum, old pal. I won't get up. It's my lumbago you know. Oh! My aching back!'

Chester the giraffe often complained of his aches and pains. He suffered from hay fever, sciatica, sleeping sickness, morning sickness, evening sickness, and lumbago. He walked with a limp and sometimes used a walking-stick to help him. Other times he leant on Boswell's brown, furry shoulder. But mostly Chester just lay on his side or sat in his arm-chair with its extra high back to support his long neck. Whenever visitors came to see him Chester would stop snoring a moment, smile, and say, 'I won't get up . . . my lumbago you know . . . mmyyyawn . . . mnmm . . . lluuuummbaayygoo,' and smile again as he returned to his favourite activity of snoring.

Boswell was too polite a teddy to ask his friend what lumbago was. It sounded awfully woody and important and smelt of pipe tobacco and medicines the way Chester said it, so Boswell thought it best not to be too curious. But tonight he felt so lonely and the rain made

him so sad that he toddled across the room on his
plump teddy-bear legs and suggested to Chester that
the two of them go to the circus to join Carlotta and the
other toys.

Chester was not im-
pressed. 'Circuses give me
hay fever and make me
sneeze,' he moaned. 'All
that straw for the horses,
and the smell of elephants
and gorillas you know, it all
makes my nose itch.'

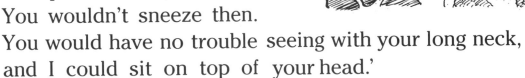

But Boswell was impa-
tient to go now. 'We could
sit up the back, Chester.
You wouldn't sneeze then.
You would have no trouble seeing with your long neck,
and I could sit on top of your head.'

Chester sighed and muttered, 'Aw! My aching back!
Aw!'

But seeing Boswell's excitement at the idea of going
to the circus he did not have the heart to say no.

'All right, Boz old buddy. We can go as long as you
don't sit on my head. You know that I suffer from a
ricked neck and with my long neck that can be very
painful.'

Boswell the bear hardly heard Chester he was so
happy. He jumped up and down and hugged Chester

around the neck. He looked like a koala holding on to a long branch of a gum tree.

Chester got to his feet slowly. He put a coloured rug on his back and tied the longest silk cravat Boswell had ever seen around his neck. 'That should keep the chill out,' he muttered, as much to himself as to Boswell. Boswell put on a teddy-bear size mackintosh and some gumboots and off they went toward the circus.

Chester limped. 'Oh! Ow! my lumbago,' he whimpered softly, but making sure Boswell heard him, as they walked. Boswell waddled along on his plump legs. He was proud of his big rubber gumboots.

'I feel like a soldier going off to war,' he told Chester excitedly.

'I feel like a soldier coming home from the war,' replied Chester with a weary moan.

The circus was not very far away. It was held in a big tent in the middle of an even bigger field in which the grass had turned brown in the summer sun. A railway line ran along one side of the field and three camels stood beside the track. Boswell waddled and Chester limped up to the ticket-booth, excited now by the sight of the camels and the sounds of the noisy crowd inside the tent.

'We would like two tickets please,' asked Boswell nicely. He held out his little paw for the tickets but the man behind the counter just looked at them.

'Tickets, my good man! Are you deaf?' Chester sternly demanded. But the man, who had a black moustache and wore a black top-hat, only stared down at them from his perch on a high stool behind the ticket counter. He looked like a nasty bird. Finally he muttered, 'No money, no tickets. Sorry, pal.'

Chester was flabbergasted; his mouth opened wide and his little giraffe's head waved about in the air. Boswell began to cry, which messed up his teddy-bear fur, and he blubbered to the mean-looking ticket seller.

'Please, mister. We only want to go under the big top. We've never been to the circus before and we have no money. We are toys!'

The bird-like man did not seem very sympathetic. But after a moment a light came into his eyes and he grinned at Chester and Boswell. He blew his purple nose and led them around the side of the tent. Twirling his black moustaches between two fat yellow fingers he talked to them in a high-pitched whisper, 'I am the ringmaster here.' He tapped his top-hat as he spoke. 'Because I like you two fellows I am going to do you a special favour and let you in for free.'

'Yippee!' cried Boswell.

'Well of course you will!' Chester exclaimed as if it were only natural that they should get in for nothing.

The ring-master led them to a hole in the tent, and, flapping his arms like a bird, ushered them inside.

Inside the tent Boswell and Chester heard clapping and cheering.

'There must be a good act on now,' Boswell said with happy anticipation.

'Yes, a couple of clowns I expect,' Chester replied in his know-all's voice. 'Now, where are our seats?'

All of a sudden the lights were very bright. Chester tripped over his long legs and knocked into Boswell as he fell down. Boswell rolled around in a circle on his back. When they finally stood up they bumped into each other because they were startled by the bright lights.

The cheers and claps grew louder. Chester said to Boswell, 'I'll lift you up. See if you can see our seats. And be careful with my neck!'

With his front legs Chester tried to hoist Boswell up on to his high shoulders. But the giraffe lost his balance and fell slowly backwards. Boswell was tossed into the air and turned three somersaults and a half before landing in a heap in Chester's lap.

The laughter and applause grew deafening.

'There must be something terrific on now, and we are missing it!' Boswell grizzled. 'What shall we do!'

'Find our seats,' said Chester as if that was as easy as pie. 'Now, you go that way Boz and I'll go this way and we can call out if one of us finds our seats.'

They set off in op-posite directions. Bos-well did not get

very far before he saw rows and rows of seats facing him. But they were all full. He turned and tod- dled back the other way. Chester did the same thing and they met in the middle and scratched their heads wondering where their seats had got to.

People laughed and laughed as the giraffe and the teddy-bear pondered this puzzle of where they were to sit. Children squealed and stamped their feet with joy and the grown- ups clapped.

Carlotta Pamplemousse jumped out of her seat with excitement at seeing two of her very own toys in the centre of the circus ring, stars of the show. Without even knowing it the two friends had been entertaining the crowd all this time. Now they bowed shyly, not sure what all the fuss was about.

The big man with the waxy moustache and the top-hat came out into the circus ring and stood between the two of them. He tried to lift their hands into the air. But Chester's legs were too long for that and when he grabbed Boswell's paw he lifted the little teddy clear off

the ground. The ring-master grinned anyway and yelled at the top of his voice.

'Tonight under the big big top at Plimpton's Circus we have been proud to present, for your enjoyment, for the first time in circus history, a giraffe and a teddy-bear team act. Ladies and gentlemen, boys and girls, let's hear it for Chester the Giraffe and Boswell the Teddy.'

The audience applauded for ages. Boswell looked around shyly, but he couldn't see anything because the lights were so bright. Chester adjusted his cravat and bowed low, his tiny head touching the saw-dust floor four metres in front of him. Carlotta Pamplemousse ran out to escort the two friends from the ring, and she was proud to take them home to her toy room.

From that day on Boswell was no longer one teddy too many. And Chester the giraffe was no longer bored by life though he still preferred to sit than stand. When visitors came to see Chester and Boswell, Chester would always say, 'I won't get up, my lumbago you know. But do let me tell you about the time Boswell and I starred in Plimpton's Circus.'

Sam's Teddy
OR
The Teddy Who Was Never Ready

Rosalind Price

Sam had a teddy. Oh yes, Sam had a teddy all right; a short, round teddy, with fearless eyes and a cheeky smile that made you want to hug him. (But Sam's teddy wouldn't stand for much hugging, except from Sam.)

Sam's teddy was just called Teddy — which may not seem like much of a name, but it suited him. A bear of few words was Teddy. He knew what he knew, and he liked what he liked, and most of the time he *did* what he liked — if he could get away with it. And often he could.

Sam's teddy could walk, and he could run — rather noisily, as a matter of fact. He could even climb up things, such as high-chairs that could topple over, and step-ladders with tins of paint on the top. He could put his pants and shirt on all by himself, but he had a bit of trouble with his shoes. And he could even sing a few songs — but you had to catch him in a good mood for that.

Everybody in the house loved Teddy — especially Sam — but he did have a few bad habits.

For one thing, he liked getting up early in the morning. Very early. Long before anyone else was awake. And of course he had to wake Sam. So then Teddy and Sam would put on their shirts, and sometimes their pants (but seldom their shoes) and stomp round the house like dinosaurs.

For another, Teddy liked to spread his toys out all over the place, to have a good look at them, but he didn't much care for putting them away again.

He liked to swoosh backwards and forwards in the bath, making the tidal waves flood over the dry land and under the bathroom door.

He liked to take all the best saucepans into the garden and use them for collecting beetles, lizards and worms.

But the most tiresome thing about Teddy was that he was never ready on time.

'Sam, come and eat your breakfast!'

'I can't. Teddy isn't ready. He hasn't put his shoes on yet.'

'Come on, Sam, we have to go to the shops.'

'Wait a bit. Teddy isn't ready. He just has to finish making this road so the trucks can come right up to the castle and the people don't have to walk outside where the dragons might get them . . .'

'Sam! Time to go back to the house! If we stay out here much longer you'll be as pink as boiled lobster.'

'But Teddy isn't ready. He's found a starfish on the rocks and it's getting all hot and it wants to be in that pool over there with its friends, and Teddy says . . .'

'I'm turning the light out, Sam, it's way past your bed-time.'

'But we haven't finished our story. Teddy isn't . . .'

'I don't care! He's *never* ready, that pesky Teddy. The light's going off *now*.'

One day, Teddy and Sam were digging in the vegetable garden when Mum called from the kitchen: 'Hey, Sam! Could you please go and shut the side gate so that Mr Next-Door's horrible dog doesn't get in? I think I left it open. I'm making a cake, and I can't stop now.'

'In a minute. Teddy isn't ready. He has to make these holes a bit bigger for the spaghetti trees. They need lots of room to grow, you know, and . . .'

And Teddy and Sam went on digging. And they forgot about the side gate.

And because they weren't ready, and didn't shut the side gate, it wasn't long before Mr Next-Door's horrible dog came sneaking through into the garden (where he knew he wasn't popular).

And because Mr Next-Door's horrible dog came snuffling round the garden, Sam's scaredy-cat, Janet, took fright and fled under the house.

And because Sam's scaredy-cat, Janet, took refuge under the house, Mum had to whip her cake into the oven and go help Sam coax Janet out.

'Here, puss, puss. Out you come, you silly old thing.'

And what do you think Mr Next-Door's horrible dog did while Sam and his mum were busy peering under the house for Janet? *It seized Teddy from the spaghetti-tree patch and ran off with him, through the side gate!*

Sam had never been so worried or upset.

He and Mum rushed into Mr Next-Door's place, but there was no sign of the horrible dog, and no sign of Teddy. Mr Next-Door came out to help them, and the three of them ran down the road towards the shop. They were just in time to see the horrible dog glance over its shoulder with a look of triumph, and squeeze into the drain by the letter-box. They soon reached the drain, but the horrible dog wriggled out the other end dragging Teddy with him.

Luckily for Teddy, the postie drew up just then in his van, leapt out, and grabbed the horrible dog by its collar.

Sam was the first to reach the postie, and there at his feet, in a puddle, was Teddy. A grubby and dishevelled Teddy, but Teddy nonetheless, and all in one piece.

Sam hugged him very tightly.

Then he and Mum took Teddy home for a clean-up, leaving Mr Next-Door to deal with his naughty, horrible dog.

When they got back to the house, they could smell the cake burning in the oven.

'What you two need is a bath,' said Mum, when she'd rescued the cake. 'Do you think Teddy's ready, for once?'

'Yes, he's ready,' said Sam quietly. 'And so am I.'

They were ready for tea, too, when Mum produced the cake (which tasted delicious with the burnt bits cut off). And they were even ready for bed on time, without being told.

Mum turned out the light and left the door slightly ajar, the way Teddy liked it.

'Perhaps we should get Teddy a watch — a bear-sized watch, with a special alarm — so that he can keep track of the time,' she said. 'What do you think?'

But Teddy wasn't ready to discuss the matter. Nor was Sam. They were asleep.

Mister Pom

Nan Hunt

Kelly had never wanted a teddy bear. She had soft toys and dolls of all kinds and shapes and went to sleep every night in a crowded bed. With her 'family' round her she had never been afraid of the dark. If she woke during the night there was always something soft and cuddly within reach.

But then her cousin Oliver who lived in the country, came to stay. 'Why do you have all them?' he asked, pointing to the soft toys.

'They're my children,' Kelly said. 'They go to bed with me every night.'

'Huh,' said Oliver. 'Catch me taking a tiger to bed!'

How do you know it doesn't come alive in the night and nibble your toes?'

'It's only a toy!' Kelly said. 'Do use your brains, Oliver.'

'Well at least I've got them,' Oliver said. 'Girls haven't. Girls only have mush in their heads. It's just as well you have me in the house. Look, you've got crocodiles and monkeys and a tartan dinosaur and a camel, even. Ooh, camels have awful teeth. Once they get a hold on you they never let go and their teeth are dirty and you get poisoning. If all your animals come alive in the night you'll wake up dead one morning, see if you don't.'

'Go away,' said Kelly. 'I hate you. I don't believe you anyway.'

'You'll be sorry!' threatened Oliver. 'When midnight strikes and they all come alive. Don't come crying to me for help then, Kelly Wallace. You're on your own. Just asking for trouble, that's what. Are you coming out to help me build a tree house?'

Kelly was so tired that night she slept very soundly. At breakfast her cousin looked at her out of the corners of his eyes and said, 'Did you hear the lions growling under your bed last night? They woke me up with all their noise.'

'Don't be stupid,' Kelly said rudely. 'There aren't any lions here.'

'That's what you think! What about the zoo?'

'They couldn't come across the water.'

'They could stow away on a ferry. Nobody's going to ask a lion for his fare, are they?'

'Stop your nonsense, children, and eat up your toast. Kelly, pass the honey to Oliver.'

'He puts his knife in it and leaves butter blobs,' Kelly said. 'He's disgusting!'

A wind began to blow just after Kelly went to bed that night. It made noises against the windows and

snapped pieces off the jacaranda. Kelly went to sleep cuddling a green crocodile. Hours later she woke up and the crocodile had gone. She groped for it and something sharp hurt her finger. 'Ooh!' Kelly sat up, wide awake, and sucked her hand. There were noises. Sneaky noises like something coming and trying not to make a sound. She dived under the sheet and hid in the comforting dark. After a while she wondered what was happening out there. Was it coming? Was it climbing up on to the bed? She moved, and there was a noise that stopped when she held her breath.

There were lions under the bed! Three, four, five, six of them, tawny gold with stiff whiskers and big, big, BIG teeth, and paws that could knock down a house. And a leopard on the wardrobe. She could see the shape of its tail hanging down over the mirror. Through the roar of a wind gust she heard the camels coming, flinging their huge feet about and baring their awful poisonous teeth at her. With a scream of fear Kelly flew out of bed and into her parents' room. She refused to go back into her own bed and spent the rest of the night cuddled down between her mother and father.

'It was the brooch in Gloria's frock that stuck in your hand last night, Kelly, see?' Her mother showed her the doll. There was a little spot of blood on it. 'Nothing was biting you. Only a pin.'

'My crocodile had gone,' Kelly said stubbornly.

'Oh, I moved that when I came in after you were asleep. It was sitting on your face.'

Oliver looked triumphant. 'Told you,' he said smugly.

'Leave the light on, Mum,' Kelly said when her mother tucked her into bed at the end of the day.

'Just for a while, then, okay?'

'Read another story,' coaxed Kelly. She chose a long one but was asleep before her mother finished reading. She woke up wondering why the light was on. Her soft toys were all as she had left them, in a row on top of the cupboard. The light made funny patterns on the ceiling. There was a blob that grew legs and scuttled across until it was right above her bed. Kelly rushed out to find

51

her father. 'There's a spider on the ceiling,' she said. 'It's going to fall on me, Dad.'

'What rubbish!' her father said. 'You're not Miss Muffet. You're Kelly Wallace, and a big brave girl.'

'Come and see,' Kelly said, tugging at his hand.

Uncle Bernard put down the book he was reading. 'Haven't you got Granddad's Beast?' he asked.

'Kelly doesn't like him,' Mr Wallace said.

'Do you know where he is? Go and get him and let me talk to Kelly for a bit.'

The Beast was a teddy bear that had belonged to Kelly's great-grandfather. He was a large bear. Most of his fur had been rubbed off and he had one brown glass eye and one blue glass eye. His nose was made of shiny

black leather and there was a stain up to his knees where he'd been sunk in the dam. Kelly looked at him with scorn. 'He's only fit for the rubbish,' she said. 'Dirty old thing.'

'Hold on there, Kelly. Wait till I tell you about him.' Uncle Bernard held Kelly on one knee and The Beast on the other and began to tell her about the adventures the teddy had been through. Then he looked Kelly in the eye and said, 'Why are you so frightened now at night? You never used to be.'

'Oliver said all my soft toys would come alive at midnight and eat me,' Kelly said. 'He said they'd get under the bed and under the door and through the keyhole if I tried to run away.'

'Oliver said! Kelly, listen to me. Oliver won't go up the hill past the dam unless someone is with him because he's so afraid.'

'*Oliver* is? In the dark, Uncle Bernard?'

'No, in broad daylight, Kelly. He says there are creatures in it.'

'Goodness!' Kelly looked up into her uncle's face. 'And are there?'

'Of course not!'

'I'm not afraid in the daytime,' Kelly said loftily.

'Now I'll tell you a secret and I'll tell you what I think you should do.' He whispered in her ear and Kelly's eyes grew rounder and rounder.

'Why is he called The Beast?' she asked, putting out a finger and touching the teddy.

'Because when he was first brought home your great-grandmother shouted, "Take that awful beast out of my sight!", that's why.'

'I don't like that name,' Kelly said. 'I'll call him Mister Pom.'

It was Mister Pom who went to bed with Kelly. She cuddled him against her while her father read her a story and afterwards Mister Pom lay staring into the dark with his one brown eye and one blue eye wide open. Late in the night Kelly woke up with a start. She was frightened. She could hear things! Suddenly she remembered what her uncle had told her. She squeezed Mister Pom's stomach hard. It wasn't a squeak that came out but a fierce deep growl.

All the lurking lions leaped up and ran away. The leopard on the wardrobe fell in a heap on the floor. The camels got their knobbly knees tangled together and all their wicked teeth fell out. The crocodiles and spiders and tigers ran round and round until they whizzed themselves into a puree.

Kelly laughed and squeezed Mister Pom again. 'Oh you are brave, Mister Pom,' she said. 'I'll never be frightened again.' And she kissed his black leather nose and went back to sleep.

Ted E. Bear, Snoozologist

Tony Lintermans

Ted E. Bear was tough, because he had to be. It wasn't easy walking into strange bedrooms every night. And when the fur on the back of his neck tingled and stood up straight because of what he might find there, in those rooms full of nightmares and crumpled beds, that was tough too. It wasn't easy to find his neck, let alone tell his fur to lie down. So he always wore an enormous overcoat, with the collar turned up, even tonight when he was alone in his office.

'*Brrr brrr.*'

He picked up the phone.

'Ted E. Bear here, snoozologist to the sleepless. You pay your dues, I'll make you snooze. What can I do for you?'

He sank back into the chair, listening as Mrs Pecker told her sad story. Often he would say, 'Uh huh', but after a while he got sick of this, and just grunted. He tired of this, too, and pulled out a small pig from his overcoat, holding it near the phone. Every time he tickled the pig, it grunted, while Ted E. Bear doodled on a pad.

'Now let me get this straight, Mrs Pecker. You've got two kids, Paula Pecker and Peter Pecker. Peter likes budgerigars and chocolate milkshakes, and sleeps like a top. Paula is seven years old, looks very much like her grandpa, and hasn't slept for two nights. And you want me to make her go to sleep?'

'Uh huh,' said Mrs Pecker over the phone.

'Tell me one thing,' said Ted. 'Are you holding a little pig up to the phone?'

'Uh huh,' grunted Mrs Pecker.

'I thought so. Now, don't you worry. I'll be over there tonight. Just leave Paula's window open.'

Ted E. Bear put down the phone and sighed. Another hard night's work ahead. He filled his pockets with the tools of his trade, and caught a taxi to Paula Pecker's place. Her bedroom was on the left side of the house. Walking softly to the window, Ted E. Bear peeked in. Paula was lying with her eyes half closed, staring at the ceiling. The clock beside her bed ticked quietly, the hour hand almost on nine.

'Hmm,' said Ted, 'she's almost asleep. A lullaby should do the trick.'

Standing right beside the open window, he started to croon his favourite lullaby, in his softest voice.

Hush little Paula, looking so sweet,
Let Ted E. Bear's voice sing you to sleep.
When you wake in the morning, Mum will be
*   pleased,*
And I'll have a fist full of sleep-maker's fees.

At least he thought it was his softest voice. Before he could sing the second verse, a big black dog stuck its head over the fence and howled. The lights next door came on, two cats started fighting, the cockatoo three doors down bashed its beak against the cage and screamed, 'Polly want silence!' and a police siren wailed in the distance. Ted E. Bear got such a fright he jumped through the window and pulled the blind down behind him!

'What was that awful noise?' asked Paula, staring wide-eyed at the strange bear in a giant overcoat.

Ted E. Bear spun round and held out his card.

'Just a dog howling and two cats fighting,' he said.

'Oh. I thought it sounded like someone singing — but no one could sing that badly.' She read the card. 'Snoozol — a snoozologist?'

'That's me, kid. And you know what that means?'

'Of course I do!' scoffed Paula. 'Snoozologists are people who sneeze in zoos.'

'Snoozologists,' said Ted, 'are sleepmakers. And in three shakes of a lamb's tail, I'll have you snoring like a whale.'

'Not me!' said Paula. 'I won't go to sleep without a —'

Her mouth dropped when she saw him pull one lamb, then another, and one more, out of his left pocket. They stood on the end of the bed.

'Lie down, lie down, Paula, they won't bite.'

Paula plumped up her pillow and lay back down as Ted E. Bear reached deep inside his overcoat and pulled out a whistle.

'I just want you to count the sheep —'

'There's three,' cried Paula quick as a whip, 'unless you've got more in your coat.'

With a sudden blow on the whistle Ted E. Bear started the lambs jumping off the bed, running round behind him, leaping back on the bed and starting again.

'Count each lap of each sheep — that'll soon put you to sleep,' Ted said.

Paula started counting. 'One, two, three, four . . .'

Ted E. Bear looked at the clock — a quarter past nine. The sheep went round and round and round, as

Paula kept counting, 'Twenty-seven, twenty-eight, twenty-nine.' At half past nine she was still counting, and at ten o'clock the lambs were like a white blur circling the very tired Ted E. Bear. Still Paula counted. 'Two hundred and forty-nine, two hundred and fifty —'

'Enough!' yelled Ted E. Bear, stopping the lambs and settling them down on the end of the bed. 'You're a tough case, kid. Even old Mrs Van Winkle's son, Rip, took me less time to put to sleep. But my next plan is foolproof.'

As Paula sat up again, waiting to see what else this funny snoozologist would do, Ted E. Bear produced a huge bag of dog biscuits from one pocket. He took a small blue feather from another pocket, and a brown labrador pup from inside the coat. Sitting the pup on the bed next to the sleeping lambs, he tied the feather to its tail, and started feeding it biscuits. Every time the labrador took a bite, he wagged his tail, and the blue feather moved from side to side.

'Okay,' said Ted. 'Count the feather each time it moves from left to right. It's guaranteed to make you sleep all night.'

'Nothing will make me sleep,' said Paula, 'except a cute, cuddly —'

'Start counting!' ordered Ted, feeding the pup. So Paula counted as the pup's tail wagged. Ted E. Bear was so sleepy that he could hardly hold his head up, but when he looked at the clock at half past ten, Paula was

still counting. 'One hundred and sixty-two, one hundred and sixty-three . . .'

At eleven o'clock Ted E. Bear's hand was wet and shiny where the labrador pup had licked and licked and licked. At twenty past eleven, he reached inside his coat for another bag of biscuits as the tail, and the blue feather, wagged and wagged and wagged. When Paula counted to two thousand three hundred and forty-four, he mumbled, 'No more!' And then *he* fell asleep!

Paula smiled and stopped counting. The labrador pup stopped wagging its tail, and went to sleep beside the lambs. Paula untied the blue feather from its tail and put it on her pillow. Then she tucked Ted E. Bear into bed, his head resting beside hers. She stroked his face, sighed, and went to sleep.

When Mrs Pecker came in next morning, she couldn't believe her eyes. Three lambs, a pup, a blue feather, a bear in bed, and Paula — all asleep!

'Paula! Wake up, you'll be late for school.'

Paula rubbed her eyes.

'Morning, Mum. I had a great sleep! All I needed was my own teddy to cuddle.'

'*Bear*!' growled a voice from under the blankets. 'The name is Ted E. *Bear*!'

'Well, Mr Bear, you're certainly a good snoozologist,' said Mrs Pecker. 'How would you like to live here all the time, so Paula sleeps every night?'

'Hmm,' said Ted, doubtful.

'Go on,' said Paula, 'I'd love you to.'

'Well,' said Ted E. Bear, sitting up and trying to scratch his neck, 'I'll need a snoozologist's fee.'

'I can't pay you money,' Mrs Pecker was firm. 'Would biscuits do?'

'Ted E. Bear biscuits?' asked Ted.

'Done,' said Mrs Pecker.

Gone-Away Bear

Libby Hathorn

I suppose when it all comes down to it, it was my fault that Amando got lost in the first place. To tell the truth Amando's been a bit difficult lately — fighting, sulking, and even hiding from me.

Last week I found two of my Star Wars dolls upside down in the fish tank and Amando sitting nearby with that angelic look on his hairy little face. He refused to admit a thing but I know very well he did it! I shook Amando until his ears waggled and then shut him in the cupboard. I know that was a bit mean but I thought he should be punished so I left him lying there among the shoes. And that was the last I saw of him — at least I think that was the last I saw of him.

You see I slept at a friend's house overnight and then when I came home I didn't really think about Amando because Anthony had bought me some new Lego and I played with that all morning. It wasn't till the afternoon that I first missed Amando. I went to the cupboard to fetch him and he wasn't there.

'Amando,' I said very sternly, 'come out from wherever you are. I know you're there, so come out at once!'

But Amando didn't come out. In fact there wasn't a sound in the room except for the gurgling of Anthony's fish tank which he lets me keep in my room now. I thought perhaps Amando was angry about being left among the shoes and was hiding in one of his familiar

64

places. I checked under the bed covers, on top of the chest of drawers and on the windowsill. No Amando to be seen. So I checked all the other places too — in the drawers, under the bed on the top of the cupboard — everywhere. But still no Amando. I asked Mum and Anthony but they hadn't seen him for ages.

'Check downstairs,' Mum suggested. 'Last time I saw Amando he was on your windowsill. He may have fallen out the window.'

I went downstairs to the yard at the back of our flats and saw Rose Epping making chalk drawings on the concrete. 'I've lost Amando,' I told her.

'Yup,' she said, not looking up from her drawing.

'Seen him?'

'Nup.'

I looked over her shoulder at the drawing she was doing. It was a human being. I couldn't tell if it was a man or a woman.

'A telly was stolen yesterday from Martin's place,' she said while heavily colouring the chalk face with bright pink stripes. 'Whoever took Martin's telly could've gone into your house and stolen Amando too.'

'Nah, Anthony works at home all day. Anthony would've heard. Anyway, Amando was hidden in the cupboard.'

Rose Epping shrugged.

'Well, where *is* he?' she asked deliberately. 'Where's Amando *now*?'

I couldn't answer so I went back upstairs and made another search of my room.

'Are you sure you didn't move Amando, Mum?' I asked.

'Quite sure,' Mum said.

'Are you sure no one's been in my room like that pesky Peter from upstairs or a robber or someone?'

'No one,' Mum said.

'No one's been here,' Anthony assured me, 'except us, and we didn't touch Amando. Don't worry, he'll turn up.'

But he didn't.

'Amando's very lonely at night if he's not on my bed,' I complained to Mum when she came to tuck me in that night.

'We'll have a really good search for Amando tomorrow,' she promised, 'and we'll find him.'

'He'll be sad without me tonight,' I told her. 'Very sad. He's probably crying right now'.

'We'll find him tomorrow,' she promised again.

Later I lay in the dark thinking about Amando somewhere lost and alone. I knew he'd have a great big lump in his throat, the kind that makes it hard to swallow. I knew he'd be brushing away a tear or two and sniffing and looking for the tissues. I couldn't find the tissues either.

Next day we hunted all through the house for Amando

but there wasn't a trace — not a whisker.

'I'll be at the shops this afternoon,' Anthony told me. 'I'll buy you a new teddy bear, just like Amando.'

'No thanks,' I said, all choked up. Anthony's awfully nice but sometimes he doesn't seem to know things, like the fact that Amando is a rare and precious bear.

'Amando's been with us always,' Mum explained to Anthony. 'You can't just go out and buy a bear like Amando.' She squeezed my hand quite hard.

'I guess we'll just have to keep looking then,' Anthony said.

'Want to come and play at my place?' It was Rose Epping at the door. 'Hide-and-seek?'

'I can't come and play,' I explained. 'I'm looking for Amando. He's still lost and I've got to —'

'Yeah, yeah,' Rose Epping cut in, 'but you can look for Amando *any time*. Let's play at my place *now*. Hide-and-seek, okay?'

Rose Epping blinked at me through her small round spectacles and I hated her at that moment waiting at the door for me to play hide-and-seek. I wasn't going to play with her now, or ever!

'No,' I said, turning away.

'Do you want a Mars Bar?' she asked. 'At my place?'

I just love Rose Epping's place, specially the kitchen cupboards. Her parents keep Mars Bars and crisps and other delicious things, and you can eat them any time.

'Yes,' I sighed, following Rose Epping over to her place. After all, a Mars Bar would give me the energy to go on looking. 'But I've got to find Amando *before* hide-and-seek.'

'Okay,' Rose Epping said, 'I'll help you find him then.'

But Rose Epping couldn't find Amando either. After we'd looked and looked we decided to play hide-and-seek after all. I didn't want to think about the coming night and just how lonely Amando was going to be without me once again.

Playing hide-and-seek with Rose Epping is great fun because she always pretends to be a very good monster when she's coming to get you and makes you very scared. You can always hear her getting closer and

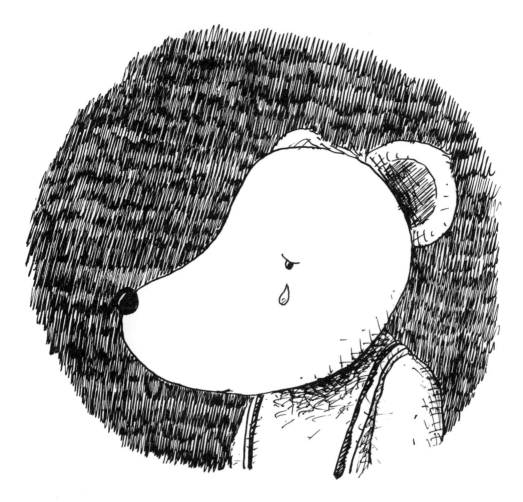

closer because she breathes so heavily. 'Coming and coming to get you,' she says in such a quiet little voice that it sends shivers up and down your back. Sometimes I have to cover my mouth and bite my fingers I want to squeal so much.

'Coming and coming to get you.' I could hear her out in the hall. I wasn't even thinking about Amando when I crawled under my bed to hide from Rose Epping.

I knew she was in the room because her breath was coming in short snorts. 'Coming and coming to get you,' she repeated in that soft little voice and I pressed up harder against the wall. I heard drawers opening and doors banging. Any minute I would see her upside-down face and her glasses shining severely as she bent over the bed intent on my hiding place.

'I'll scream,' I thought. 'I'll scream out loud.'

And I stuffed my hand in my mouth as Rose Epping jumped on the bed and slowly lifted the sheet that dangled down and hid me.

'Coming and coming to —'

But before she could finish, before she even saw me, I yelled so loud it was Rose Epping who jumped.

'AMANDO!' I yelled. 'Amando, Amando, Amando's here!'

The sheet went up quickly, her upside-down face appeared and it wasn't frightening at all!

'*You* said you *looked* under your bed for Amando,' she glared.

'I did. We all did. But look where he is!'

I waggled an orange hairy paw that hung down now between the wooden slats of my bedbase.

'You can't see him unless you're lying right *under* here. He got under my mattress somehow. Quick, help me get him out or he could be squashed to death.'

One thing about Rose Epping, she always knows when it's an emergency, and she helped me get the mattress off the little bear very quickly. We checked for broken bones but Amando was quite okay. And he was *awfully* glad to see me.

'Hey, Mum. Hey, Anthony,' I called. 'Hey, anybody! I've found Amando! We've found Amando! Hey! Hey!' I was awfully glad too.

That night, after Anthony and Mum had kissed me goodnight, I had a long serious talk with Amando. We both promised that we would never be mean to each other again and I promised especially that I would never put him in my cupboard or in any other cupboard for that matter. Amando hugged me very tight and I even had to brush away a tear or two from his hairy little face. He was so glad to be back with me, safe and sound. I stroked his forehead and his soft leather nose and I knew he'd fall asleep in no time.

'Am I glad to see you!' I said to Amando over and over again until Mum called out from down the hall.

'For heaven's sake, go to sleep!'

Then I gave Amando an extra big hug and I did!